How to Catch a Star

Oliver Jeffers

Once there was a boy

and the boy loved stars very much.

Every night the boy watched
the stars from his window

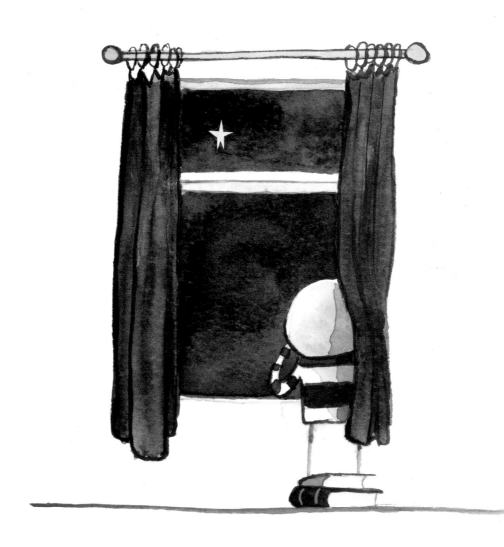

and wished he had one of his very own.

He dreamed how this star might be his friend.
They would play hide-and-go-seek

and take long walks together.

The boy decided he would try to catch
a star. He thought that getting up early
in the morning would be best,

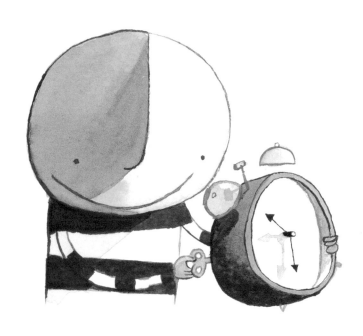

because then the star would be tired
from being up in the sky all night.

So, the next day he set out at sunrise.

But he could not see a star anywhere.
He sat down and waited for one to appear.

He waited...

and he waited...

and ate lunch...

...and waited.

And after
dinner

he waited some more.

Finally, just before
the sun was about to
go away, he saw a star.

The boy tried to
jump up and grab it.

But he could not
jump high enough.

So, very carefully,
    he climbed to the
        top of the tallest
            tree he could find.

But the star was still way out of reach.

He thought he might
lasso the star with
the life belt
from his
father's
boat.

But it was much too heavy
for him to carry.

He thought he could fly up in his spaceship and just grab the star. But his spaceship had run out of petrol last Tuesday when he flew to the moon.

Perhaps he could get a seagull to help
him fly up into the sky to reach his star?

But the only seagull he could find
didn't want to help at all.

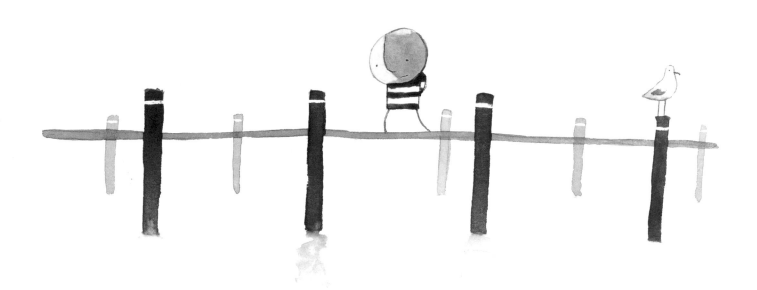

The boy thought he would
never catch a star.

Just then he noticed something floating in the water. It was the prettiest star he had ever seen. Just a baby star. It must have fallen from the sky.

He tried to fish the star out with his hands.

But he couldn't reach it.

Then he had an idea.
The star might wash up on the shore.
He ran back along the jetty to the beach.

Then he waited and walked...

...and watched and waited...

... and, sure enough,

the star washed up on the bright, golden sand.

The boy had caught a star.

A star of his very own.

For Marie and Paul

First published in hardback in Great Britain by HarperCollins Children's Books in 2004
First published in paperback in 2005

Text and illustrations copyright © Oliver Jeffers 2004

ISBN-13: 978-0-00-715034-2

15 17 19 20 18 16

Cover design by Rory Jeffers

Visit our website at: www.harpercollins.co.uk

Printed and bound by Printing Express, Hong Kong

HarperCollins *Children's Books*